This Book
Belongs to

To COREY

LOVE AUNTIE EVELYN   6/02/05

Disney's
Easy-to-Read
TREASURY

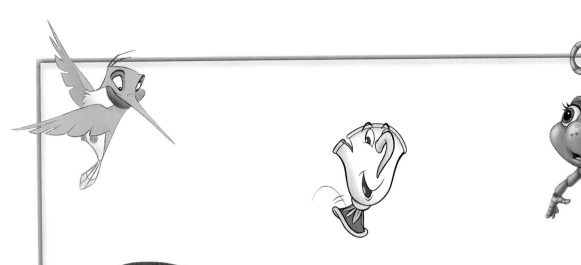

Disney's
Easy-to-Read
TREASURY

Disney PRESS

New York

Disney's
Easy-to-Read
TREASURY

C O N T E N T S

BUZZ AND THE
BUBBLE PLANET

by Judy Katschke

There was a new toy in Andy's room.

"It looks like a spaceship,"

said Woody.

"Did you say 'spaceship'?"

Buzz asked.

Buzz got in the spaceship.

Woody told Buzz to be careful.

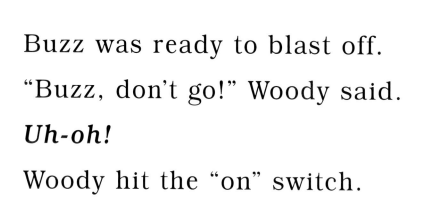

Buzz was ready to blast off.

"Buzz, don't go!" Woody said.

Uh-oh!

Woody hit the "on" switch.

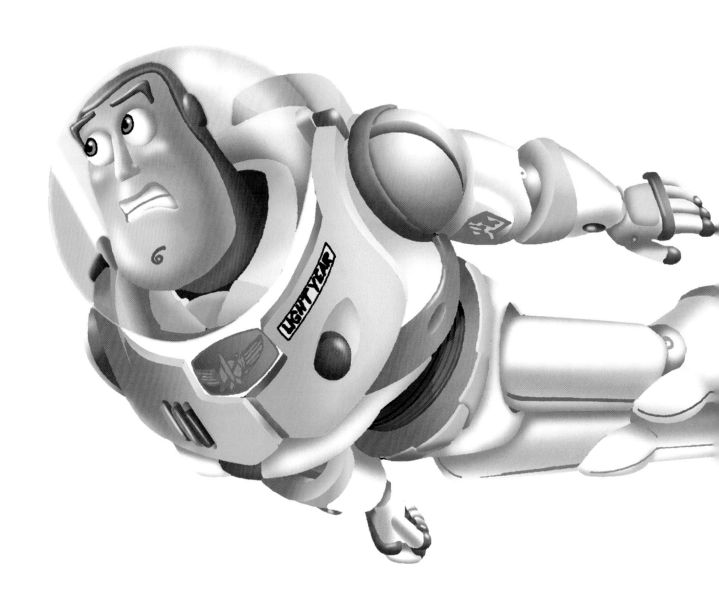

Whoosh!

The spaceship went
up, up, and away!
Then it came down.
Buzz fell out.

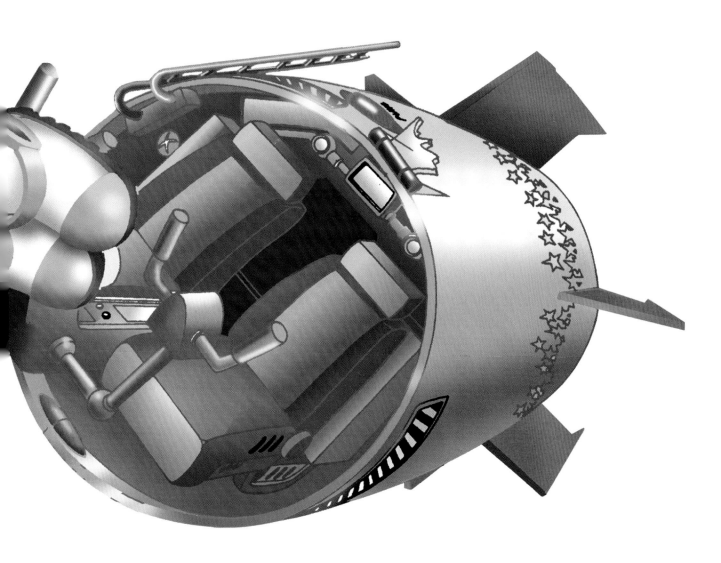

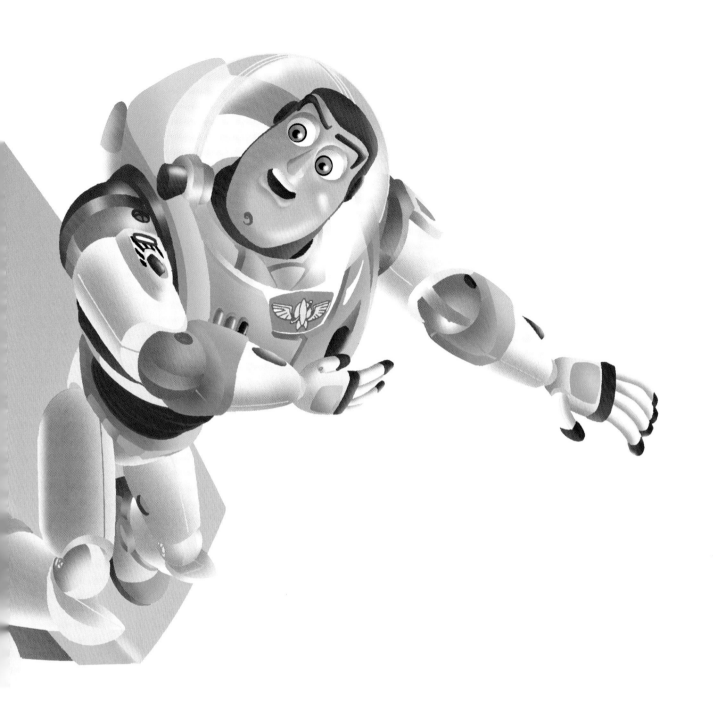

Buzz landed in some water.

He jumped out.

The water went down.

"I am on a strange planet,"
said Buzz.
"I must look around.
After all, I *am* Buzz Lightyear!
But how will I get home?"
he said.

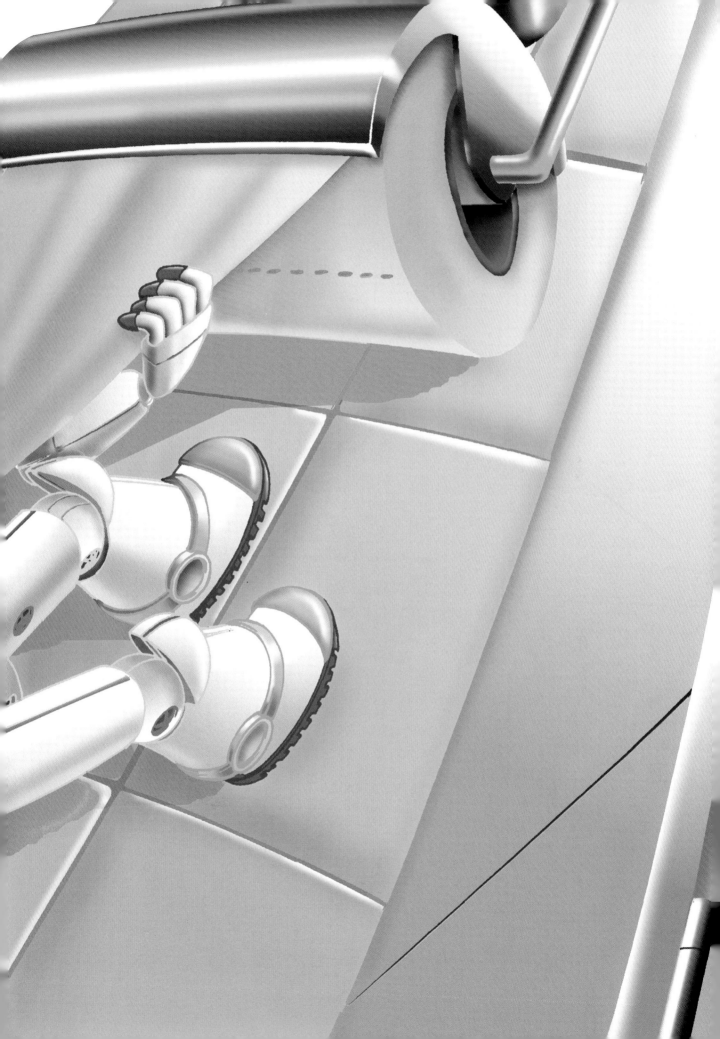

Back in Andy's room,
the toys held a meeting.
"We must find Buzz," said Woody.
"I will send out
the Green Army Men," said Sarge.
"Great idea!" said the toys.

Buzz was in trouble.

A robot was pushing him.

It shook in his hands.

Buzz could not hold on.

He hit a button.

The robot stopped.

Next, strong winds
pushed Buzz.

He slipped on a rock.

He got covered in blue slime.

Buzz saw Andy's cat, Whiskers.

"Do not worry, Whiskers.

I will rescue you," he said.

The cat's tail swung at Buzz.

THUMP!

Buzz was in a red boat.

"This planet moves
too much," said Buzz.

Buzz saw yellow aliens.

They swam to him.

"Who is your leader?"

Buzz called.

"Squeak," said the yellow aliens.

Buzz's wings opened.

His wings hit a bottle of

SQUEAKYCLEAN BUBBLES.

"You must be Squeak," Buzz said.

"I am Buzz Lightyear. I come in peace."

Thick pink goo

came out of Squeak's head.

The goo turned into lots of bubbles.

Buzz slapped the bubbles.

But they were all around him.

Sarge and his men saw Buzz.

Sarge called Woody.

"Should we save him?" he asked.

"Do not worry," said Woody.

"Help is on the way!"

Back on the Bubble Planet,
Buzz was in trouble again.
Aliens were all around him.
Soon he would fall
into Squeak's bubble trap.

At last, help came.

Andy was on the Bubble Planet.

And Andy had Woody.

"Let's go, partners!" Andy said.

The Bubble Planet was
not so scary anymore.
Buzz was happy.
His friends were here.
And he was clean!

47

DISNEY'S

THE
LION KING

ROAR!

by Patricia Grossman

The day begins.

Simba and Nala say hello.

Then they start to roar.

Simba roars at the tall giraffes.

The giraffes chew the grass.

They toss their heads.

Nala roars at the monkeys.

They are busy.

The monkeys just laugh at Nala.

Simba roars at the big elephants.

They are not afraid.

The elephants just trumpet back.

Nala roars at the zebras.

The zebras do not look up.

They just keep eating.

Simba and Nala see Zazu.

Zazu is napping high in a tree.

Now Simba and Nala

can have some fun!

Simba roars at Zazu.

Simba's roar is loud!

Zazu keeps napping.

He does not hear Simba.

Nala roars at Zazu.

Nala's roar is loud!

Zazu does not hear Nala, either.

He just keeps dreaming.

Simba roars louder at Zazu.

Zazu still does not wake up.

He just snores.

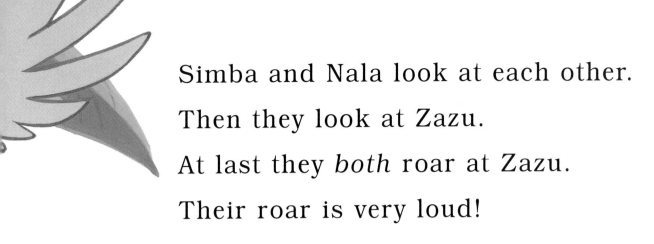

Simba and Nala look at each other.

Then they look at Zazu.

At last they *both* roar at Zazu.

Their roar is very loud!

Good-bye, nap.

Good-bye, dreams.

Good-bye, snores.

"Go roar somewhere else!"

shouts Zazu.

Nala and Simba just laugh!

Aladdin

Abu Monkeys Around

by Anne Schreiber

Every Monday,

when the week began,

to Sunday, at its end,

Abu played tricks on the Genie

and all of the Genie's friends.

On Monday,

everyone was sleeping.

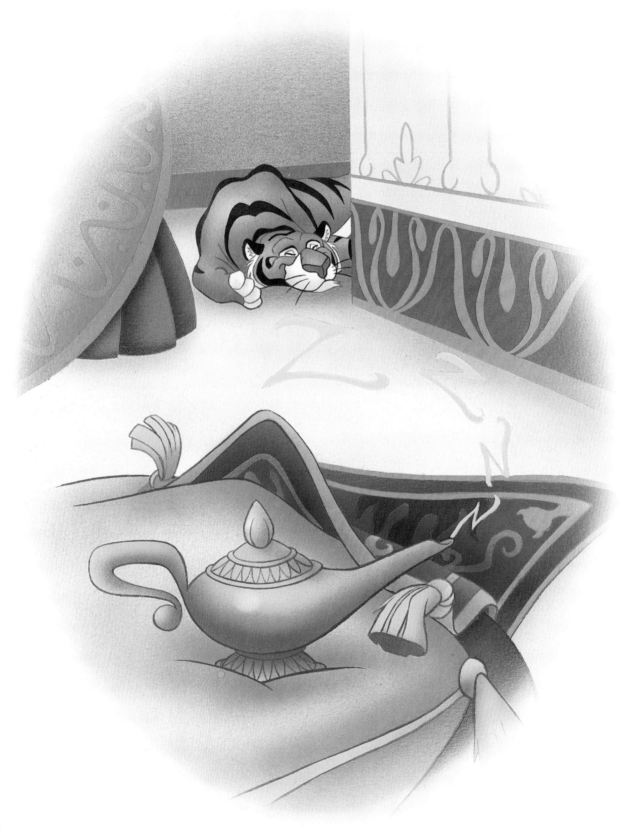

Except Abu.

BANG!

Abu banged the lamp.

It started to shake.

It fell on the floor.

Was the Genie awake?

On Tuesday,

the Genie was combing.

But not Abu.

CLANG!

Abu scared the Genie
by ringing a bell.
The Genie jumped up.
Down Abu fell.

On Wednesday,
everyone was eating.

Except Abu.

CRASH!

Abu spilled the juice.

He dropped the fruit.

The Genie got juice
all over his suit.

On Thursday,

everyone was resting.

Except Abu.

SPLASH!

Abu jumped into the water.

He wanted to swim.

Aladdin got wet.

The Genie fell in.

On Friday,

everyone was shopping.

Except Abu.

WHOOSH!

Abu left a mess
on the ground.
His friends walked by
and slid all around.

On Saturday,

everyone was working.

Except Abu.

SWOOSH!

Abu jumped up
to grab a sweet treat.
He knocked a basket over.
Apples rolled down the street.

What has Abu done?

On Monday he woke the Genie.

On Tuesday he made things crash.

On Wednesday he spilled the juice.

On Thursday he made a splash.

On Friday he left a mess,

and all his friends fell down.

On Saturday he jumped on a fruit stand,

and spilled apples on the ground.

On Sunday, when the
week was through,
no one could sleep.

Except Abu.

ZZZZZZZZZZZ.

What's That Noise?

by Carol Pugliano-Martin

It was a dark night.

Lady and Tramp were alone
in the house.

Suddenly, Lady heard a noise.

"What's that noise?" Lady asked Tramp.

"The floor is making that noise,"

said Tramp.

Lady was not so sure.

But Tramp said,

"Lady, we are safe and sound.

I am the bravest dog around!"

Tramp shut his eyes.

But Lady could not sleep.

"I must watch the house!"

she said.

Then Lady heard another noise.
She shook Tramp.
"What's that noise?" Lady asked.

"That noise is just the wind,"
said Tramp.

"Lady, we are safe and sound.
I am the bravest dog around!"

Lady heard another noise!

Bang! Crash!

Who was outside the house?

"What's that noise?"
Lady asked Tramp.
Tramp said,
"That is just thunder.
Lady, we are safe and sound.
I am the bravest dog around!"

"I hope you are right," Lady said.

Lady heard another sound.

Plink! Plink!

Was there someone **inside** the house?

Lady ran to the kitchen
and barked.
Tramp ran in.

"What's that noise?" Lady asked.

"That noise is the rain
falling into the pot," Tramp said.

Tramp said,

"Lady, we are safe and sound.

I am the bravest dog around!"

Lady heard the windows shake.

Then she heard a loud bark.

"Ruff! Ruff! Ruff!"

It was Tramp!

Tramp was looking at
a big shadow on the wall.
"What is that?" Tramp asked Lady.
Lady had to find out what it was.

Lady said, "I must be brave."
She looked at the rug.
The big shadow was
a teeny, tiny bug!

Tramp was still on the piano.

"Do not be afraid," Lady said.

"It is a teeny, tiny bug."

"I was not afraid," Tramp said.

"Tramp, you were right," Lady said.

"We *are* safe and sound."

"That's right," Tramp said.

"We are the bravest dogs around!"

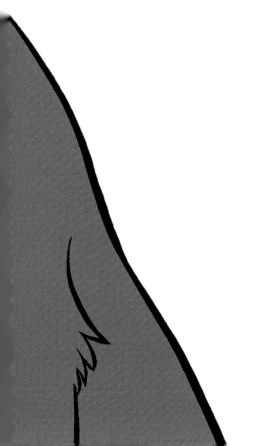

Lost!

by Kathryn Cristaldi McKeon

Mulan was hot and tired.

She was a soldier.

It was hard work.

Yao made fun of Mulan.
"That skinny guy is
one strange bird," he said.
Ling and Chien-Po laughed.

Mulan, Yao, Ling, and Chien-Po
shot arrows.

They needed to practice.

Mulan shot an arrow at a tree.

TWANG!

The arrow came
very close to Yao's hair.

"I guess my aim is a little off,"
Mulan said in a deep voice.

Yao's face was red.

He grabbed Mulan's arrow.

He shot the arrow into the woods.

"You'd better get that," Yao told Mulan.

"You need more practice."

"Wait for me," Mulan said.

"We will wait here," they said.

Mulan and Mushu
walked into the woods.

They walked for a long time.

They did not see the arrow.

Mushu was worried.

"Where are we?" he asked.

Mulan looked to the right.

She looked to the left.

She called her friends.

But no one answered.

"We are lost!" said Mushu.

Mushu leaned back on a tree.

The tree was soft and warm.

The tree was furry!

"Hey, this tree is not a tree!" said Mushu.

"No, it is a giant panda bear!"

Mulan cried.

"Help!" said Mushu.

Mulan saw a bamboo tree.

She grabbed some leaves.

Panda bears love bamboo leaves.

He sat down and ate them.

Mulan and Mushu were still lost.

"Maybe this swamp meets up

with the lake near our camp," said Mulan.

Mushu climbed onto a log.

"Mushu," said Mulan.

"That log has a lot of teeth."

Mushu was standing

on a giant alligator!

"Aaaah!" he screamed.

"Help!" Mushu shouted.

Mulan grabbed some reeds.

She waved the reeds in the air.

"You are getting very sleepy,"

she told the alligator.

The alligator fell asleep.

"I was getting dizzy," said Mushu.

"I knew you were a dizzy dragon!"
Mulan said.

Mulan and Mushu were still lost.

"Where is our camp?" asked Mushu.

"I think I can see it," said Mulan.

When they got close to the camp,
they heard crying and snarling.
Yao, Ling, and Chien-Po were
surrounded by wolves.
The wolves were snarling.
The men were crying.

"Good-bye, world!" said Chien-Po.

Yao covered his eyes.

"I want my mommy!" said Ling.

Mulan had an idea.

She hid behind a tree.

"Aaaooo!" she cried. *"Aaaooo!"*

The wolves howled at the moon.

The men walked away.

They did not see Mulan.

Back at camp Yao told what happened.
"A pack of monster wolves
surrounded us," he said.
"But we showed them
who was boss," said Ling.

"You guys are so brave," Mulan said.
"Those wolves would make me
cry for my mommy."
Then she smiled at Mushu.

Disney's THE LITTLE MERMAID

Ariel and the Very Best Book

by Patrick Daley and Joan Michael

"Where is Ariel?"
asked the King of the Sea.
Sebastian said,
"She is reading again.
Come with us
and you will see."

King Triton scolded Ariel.
"Why must you read
all day and all night?
Books are for people.
This just is not right."

"But, Father, I will show you
how great books can be.
I will show you my best books.
Then you will see."

"Look, Father, look.
Look at this book.
It has pictures and maps
and places to go.
There are wonderful places.
These are places to know."

King Triton frowned.
"A book full of maps?
That is no good to me.
I have no need for maps.
I live in the sea!"

Ariel tried again.

"Look at this book.

It is full of fish.

It tells all about them.

It tells all you wish."

"A book about fish?
That is no good to me.
I know all about fish,"
said the King of the Sea.

"I will find you a book,"
Ariel said with a smile.
"I will find a book.
But it may take a while."

"I will draw and I will write.
I will cut and I will color.

I will make him a book
that is like no other."

Said the King of the Sea,
"What is this book
you are giving to me?
It tells all about
our life in the sea!
Yes, this is a good book.
I have to agree."

"It is the very best book,"
said the King of the Sea.
"Would you like to read it?
Would you read it to me?"

Chip's Favorite Season

by Patrick Daley

It's here! It's here!

Today is the day.

What will we tell him?

What will we say?

Wake up, Chip.

It's time to play.

Winter is here.

What do

you say?

Slide down the hill.

Skate on the ice.

I like winter.

It's so nice!

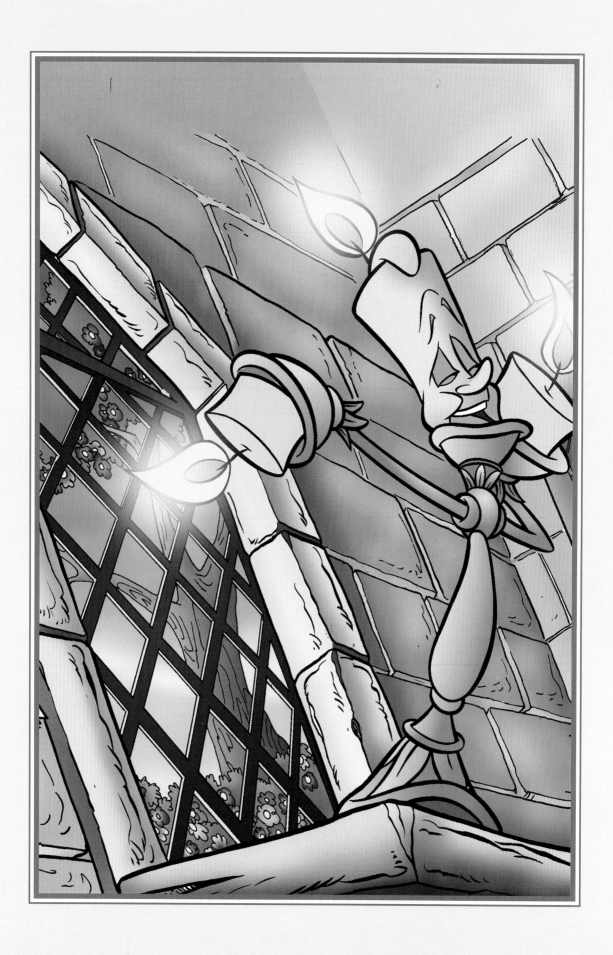

Wake up, Chip.

It's time to play.

Spring is here.

What do you say?

Jump in the mud.

Make a mess.

I like spring.

It's the best!

Wake up, Chip.

It's time to play.

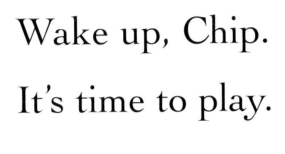

Summer is here.

What do you say?

Swim in the pond.

Play in the sun.

I like summer.

It's so much fun!

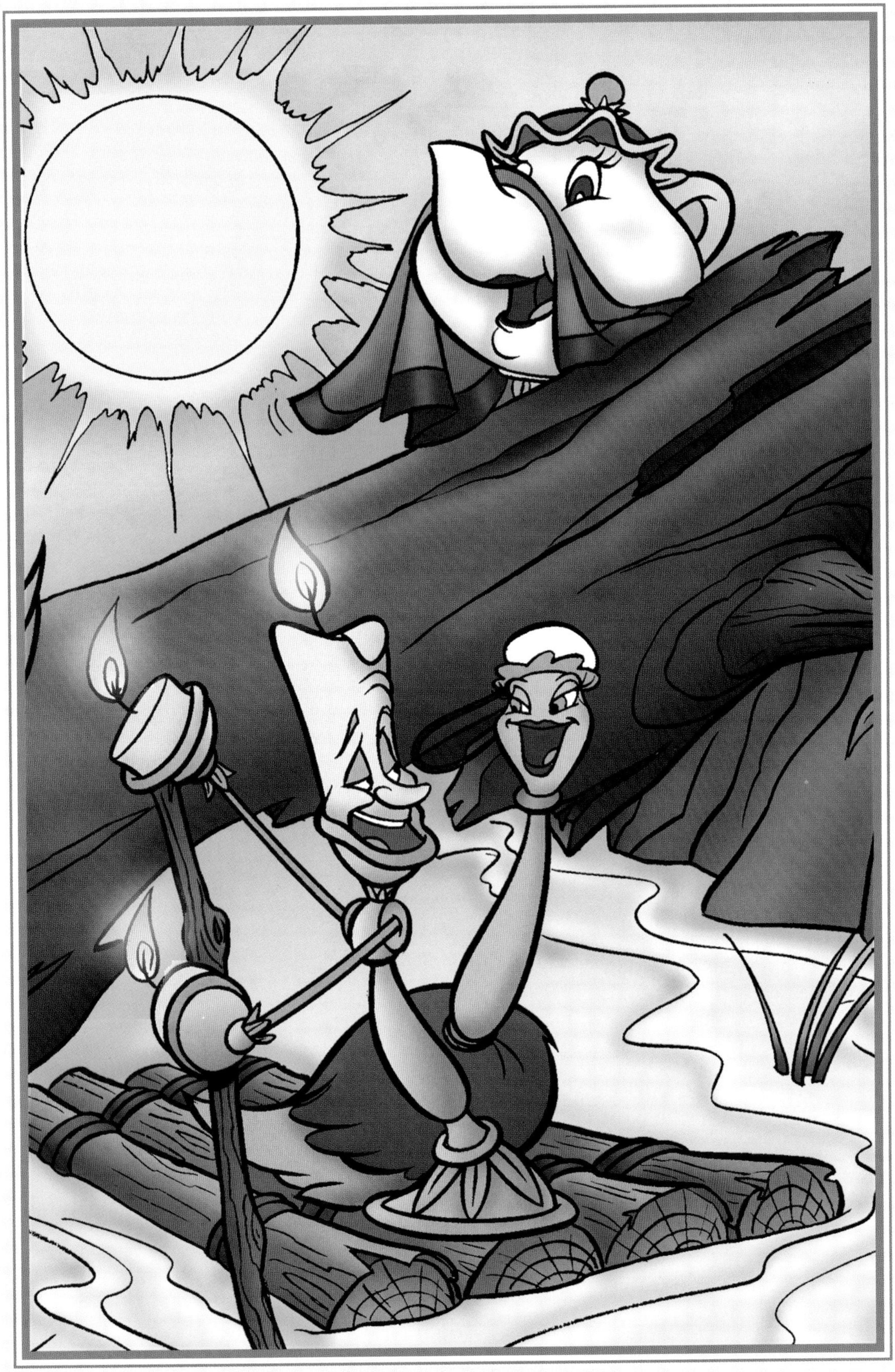

Wake up, Chip.

It's time to play.

Fall is here.

What do you say?

Rake all the leaves.

Jump in the pile.

I like fall.

It makes me smile.

Winter.
Spring.
Summer.
Fall.

Chip likes the seasons.

He likes them all.

Flik's Perfect Gift

by Judy Katschke

It is Queen Atta's
birthday.

All the ants are
bringing gifts!

But what's bugging Flik?

"I want to bring
the perfect gift!"
Flik said.

Flik looked high.

Flik looked low.

Finding the perfect
gift is no picnic!

Flik thought

and thought.

"I've got it!"

he cried.

Flik's ideas
started to bloom!

"It's just a plain
old daisy now,"
Flik said to Dot.

"But soon it will be . . .
a merry-go-round for Atta!

Come on, Dot,

let's try it out!"

WHOOPS!

"Maybe Atta can use

a nice, cool breeze!

Get ready to

CHILL, Dot!"

WHOOSH!

"Or how about a new way for Atta to fly?

Hop on, Dot!"

WHOAA!

"Maybe you should just get Atta a card," Dot said.

"No!" Flik cried.

"I *will* find the perfect present!"

"I will build her a beach
umbrella!" Flik said.
"A sprinkler!
A Ferris wheel!"

Uh-oh. It's Queen Atta!

"What's that, Flik?"

Queen Atta asked.

"It's just a plain old daisy," Flik said.

"It's perfect!" Queen Atta cried.

"It is?" Flik asked. He looked at the daisy and smiled. "IT IS!  Happy birthday, Atta!"

Where's Flit?

by Bettina Ling

"Let's go see Grandmother Willow," Pocahontas called to Flit and Meeko. "There is the path. Come on, let's go."

As Meeko led the way,
Pocahontas stopped to say,
"Where's Flit?"

Here's a
good place to hide.
Pocahontas
looked inside.

No Flit.

Pocahontas
looked in a tree.
What's up there?
Whose nest did
she see?

Not Flit's.

Meeko heard a sound.

He looked all around.

Still no Flit.

Is Flit down a hole?

Or inside the log?

Or is he in the mud
with a tiny frog?

Where else can they look?

Where else can they go?

Maybe Grandmother

Willow will know.

Pocahontas said, "Where's Flit?"

Look who they see in the old willow tree?

It's Flit!

Genie School

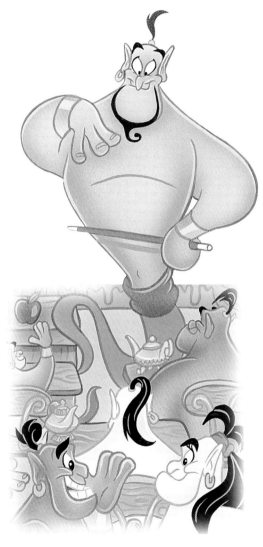

by K. A. Alister

"Last one to the palace is a rotten egg," said Jasmine.

Suddenly, a blue genie appeared before Aladdin and Jasmine.

"Does someone
want
eggs?"
Genie
asked.

"Thanks, Genie,"
Aladdin said.
Before Aladdin
could take a bite,
Abu grabbed the plate.

Abu handed Aladdin
the empty plate.

"Thanks, Abu,"
Aladdin said.
"You are more fun
than a barrel of monkeys."

Genie
snapped his
fingers. A
big barrel
appeared.

Monkeys popped out of the barrel and began to sing and dance.

Abu did not join in. The monkeys took a bow. In a flash, the barrel was gone.

"Where did you learn that trick?" asked Jasmine.

"In genie school," said Genie. "Close your eyes and I'll take you."

He snapped his fingers and said, "KA-ZAM!"

Aladdin and Jasmine were sitting in a very strange classroom.

There were yellow genies, red genies, purple genies, and even a teeny-weeny green genie.

"Good morning, class," said Genie.
"Today we are going to talk about
appearing and . . ."

But before Genie could say
"disappearing," all the genies
disappeared!

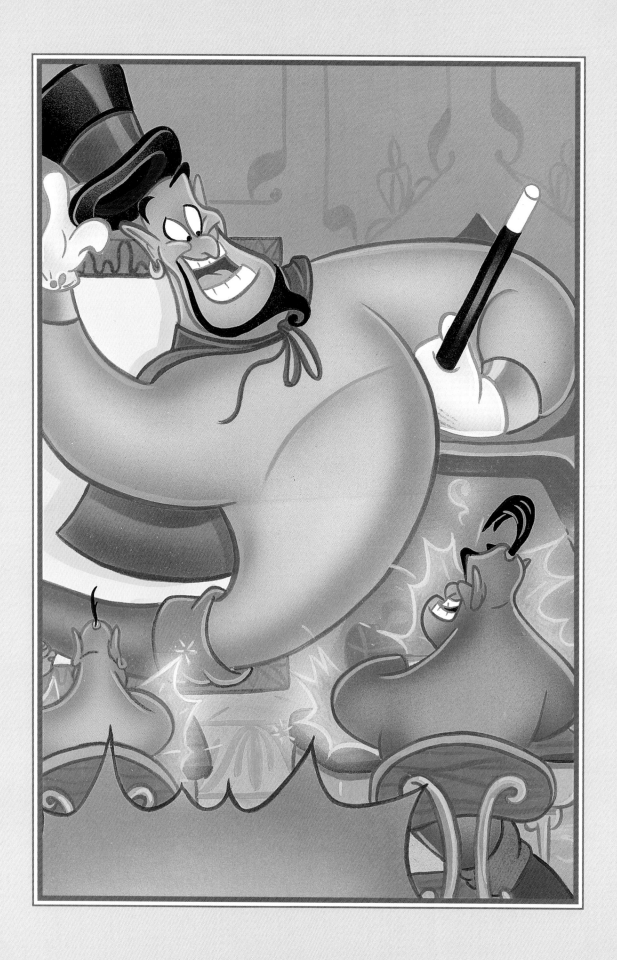

A moment later they all came back.

"Bravo! Bravo!" Genie said proudly.

"I guess he wasn't kidding about genie school," Jasmine said to Aladdin.

A nanny goat and
her three kids appeared.
They erased the chalk-
board with their tails.
When it was clean,

Genie made the

goats disappear.

"Now, let's do some math," said Genie.

"Math!" groaned the teeny-weeny green genie. "Who needs math?"

"We give out three wishes," said Genie. "No more, no less."

"If you do not learn your numbers, your work will never be done," Genie said.

"Now, count along with me," said Genie.

"One . . . two . . . three!"

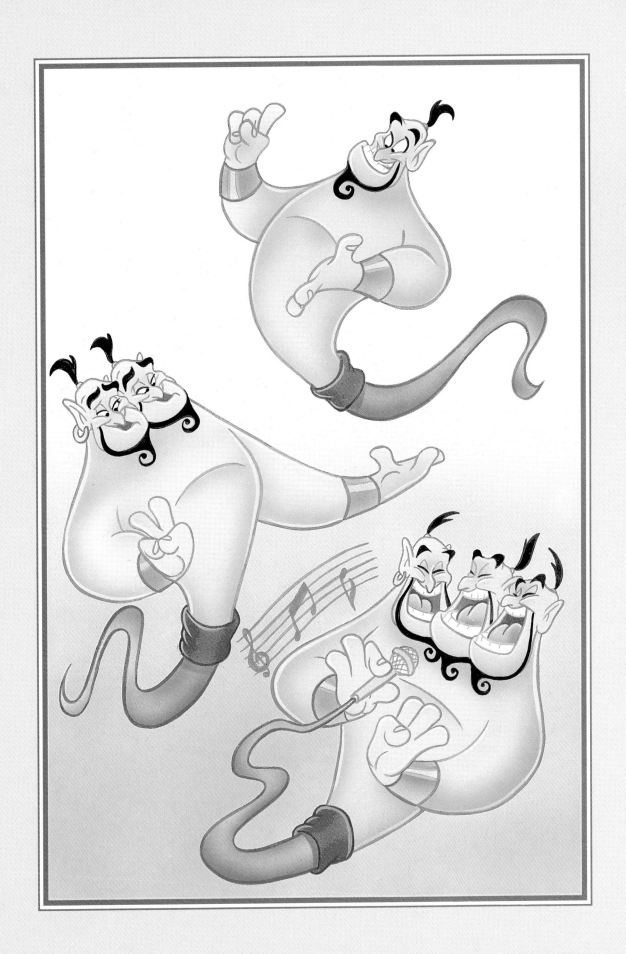

When their math lesson
was over, the little genies
had some milk and cookies.

"I also know a few
tricks," Aladdin said.

He ate his third cookie.

"Really?" Jasmine said.
"Show me."

"You just saw one," said Aladdin. "I made three yummy cookies disappear."

"That is your trick?"
Jasmine said. "I can
top that. I can grow
a mustache."

Jasmine drank a glass
of milk.

"KA-ZAM!" she said.

After snacks, it was
time for a nap.
All of the genies
disappeared into
their lamps.

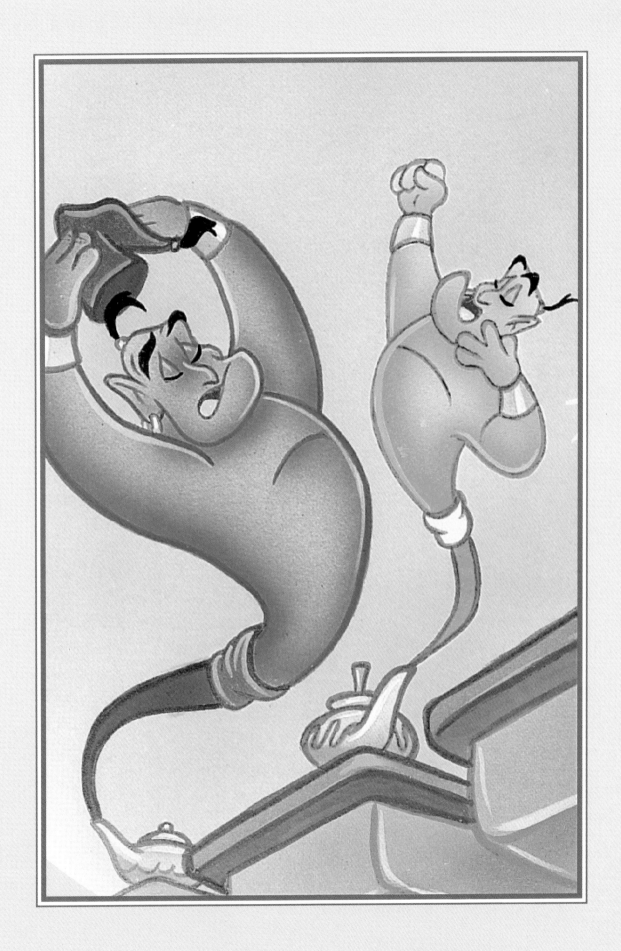

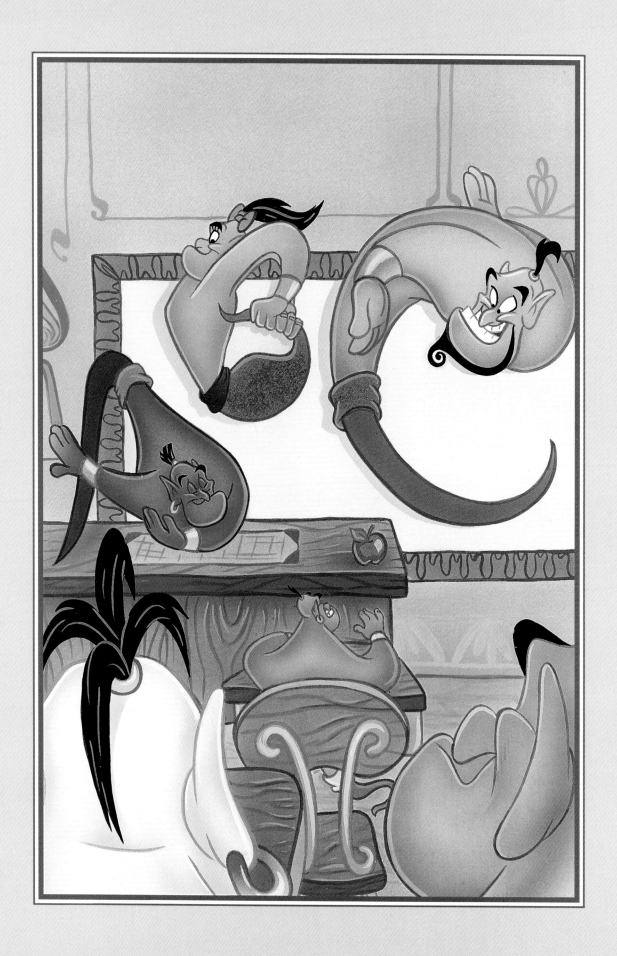

When the genies woke
up, they were ready to
learn their ABCs.

"A is for apple,"
said a red genie.

He snapped his fingers.

An apple
appeared on
his desk.

"B is for banana,"
a yellow genie said.
She snapped her
fingers, and a banana
appeared.

At three o'clock, the
bell rang.

"School's out!"
cried Genie.

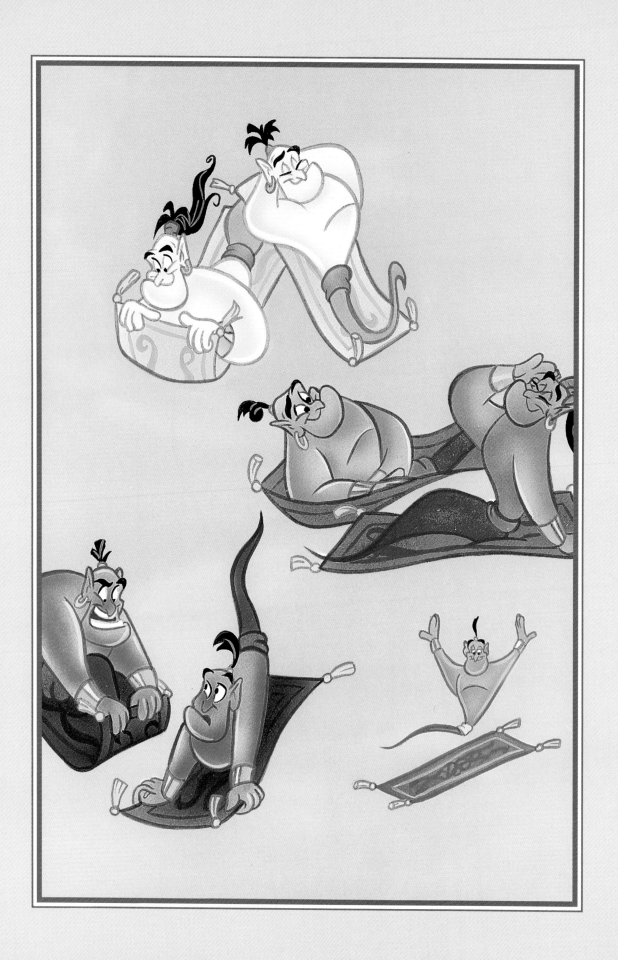

The yellow genies got on yellow carpets.

The red genies got on red carpets.

The purple genies got on purple magic carpets, and the teeny-weeny green genie got on his teeny-weeny green carpet.

"How will we get home?" asked Aladdin.

"We don't have a magic flying carpet," said Jasmine.

"KA-ZAM!" cried Genie.

Back in Agrabah,
Aladdin wanted to try
some tricks.

"Get ready, Abu,"
said Aladdin. "B is
for banana!"

Aladdin snapped his
fingers.

Nothing happened.

Genie appeared.

He handed Abu a bunch

of bananas.

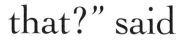

"Why can't I do

that?" said

Aladdin.

"I went

to genie

school."

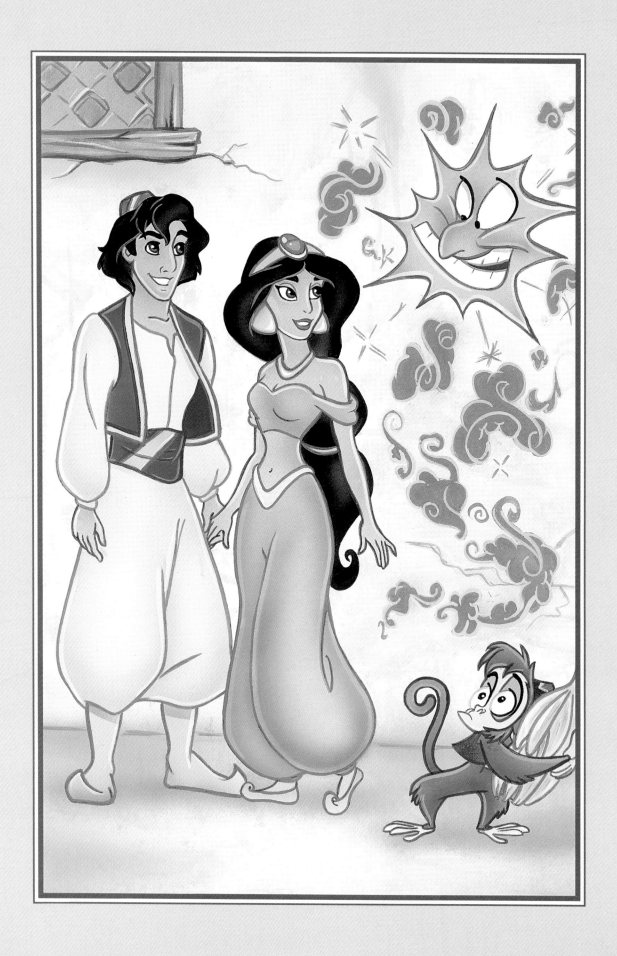

"Al, my pal," said Genie, "appearing and disappearing is for genies only."

And Genie waved good-bye . . .

. . . and disappeared!

Simba's
Pouncing Lesson

by Gail Tuchman

In the jungle
of monkeys and trees,
and swinging vines,
and a cooling breeze,
came a cry from Timon.
"Eeeeee-yaaaa!
Charge . . . Pumbaa!"

"What are you doing,
kid?" Pumbaa asked.

"Pouncing," said Simba,
"but I missed."

"Timon," said Pumbaa.
"Let's help our cub.
He needs a lesson
in getting some grub."

"Here's how to pounce,"
Timon pointed out,
as he tiptoed about
on Pumbaa's snout.
  "First, tiptoe,
nice and slow.
Then, pounce.
Ready, set, GO!"

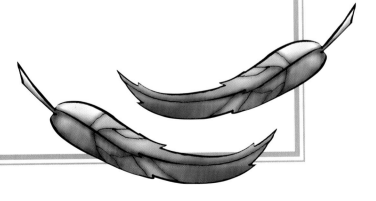

"Okay," said Simba.

"I will give it a shake.

Watch me pounce

on that big snake."

Simba said to himself,

First, tiptoe, nice and slow.

Then, pounce.

Ready, set,

GO!

In the jungle of
monkeys and trees,
and swinging vines,
and a cooling breeze,
Simba missed.

The snake hissed.

"This time,"
said Pumbaa,
"pretend you are a spy
and follow that fly.
Creep close,
then leap high."

"Okay," said Simba.
"I will give it a try.

I will pretend

I'm a spy

and follow that fly.

Creep close,

then leap high."

In the jungle

of monkeys and trees,

and swinging vines,

and a cooling breeze,

Simba SNEEZED.

The fly flew away.

Simba wasn't pleased.

"Try again, kid," Timon called out, as he bounced about on Pumbaa's snout.

"It's the bounce that counts when you want to pounce!"

Simba thought
of what his father had said.
"Stay low to the ground,
and don't make a sound."
So Simba quietly
practiced
pouncing
around.

Pumbaa and Timon were sniffing for ants. Simba hid and watched from behind some plants.

The lion cub stayed low to the ground, and without making a sound . . .

. . . Simba pounced.

"GOTCHA!" he proudly
announced.

"Good surprise, kid,"

said Pumbaa with a groan.

"Great pouncing," moaned Timon.

In the jungle
of monkeys and trees,
and swinging vines,
and a cooling breeze,
came a cry.
   "Eeeeee-yaaaa!
HOORAY . . . Simba!"

To School
and Beyond

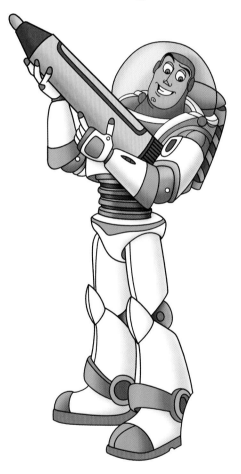

by Judy Katschke

"What is Andy doing?"
Buzz asked.

"It's the hundredth day
of school," said Woody.

"Andy is bringing in one
hundred toys for show-
and-tell."

The toys were happy that Buzz and
Woody were chosen to go to school.

"You have been chosen!"

the alien said.

"School sounds like a strange planet," Buzz said. "What if I do not like it there?"

"You will," Woody said.

Sarge got his troops marching.

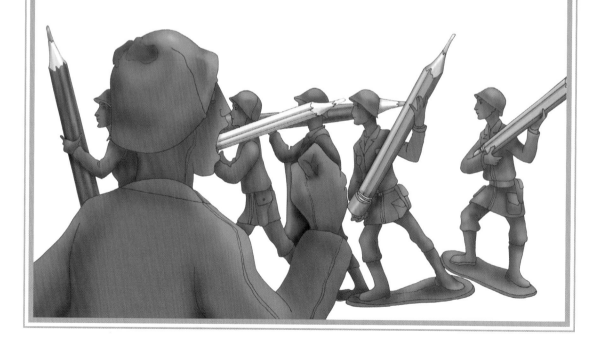

357

At school Andy put his
backpack in his cubby.
Buzz and Woody
peeked out of the backpack.
Buzz hopped out.

"I think I will like it here," Buzz said.

Woody ran after Buzz. "Get back in that pack!" Woody said. "Andy needs us for show-and-tell!"

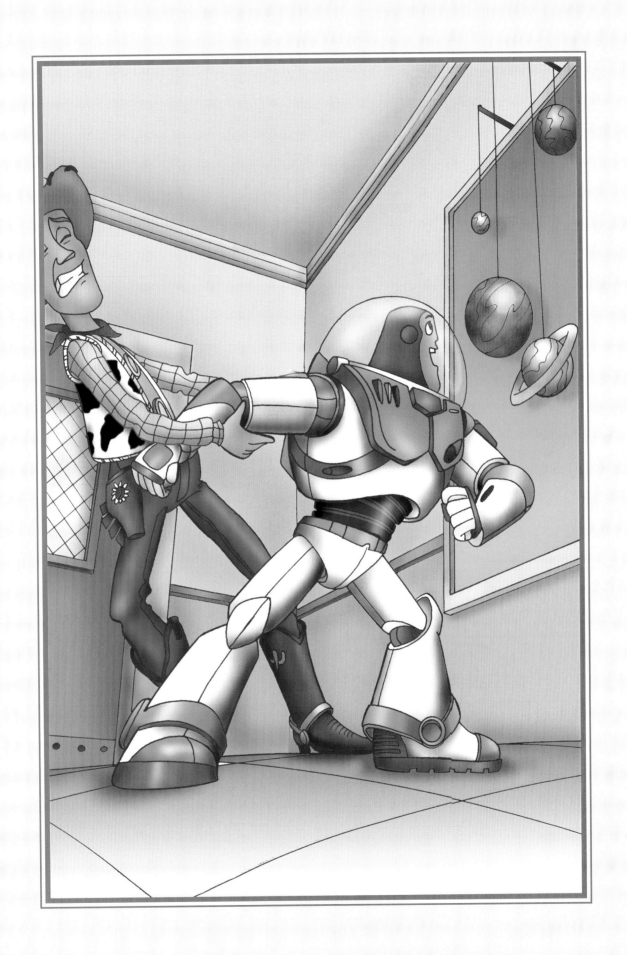

Buzz ran down the
hall. Woody followed
him.

Buzz looked into
a classroom.

"No, Buzz,"
Woody said. "That
is not Andy's class.

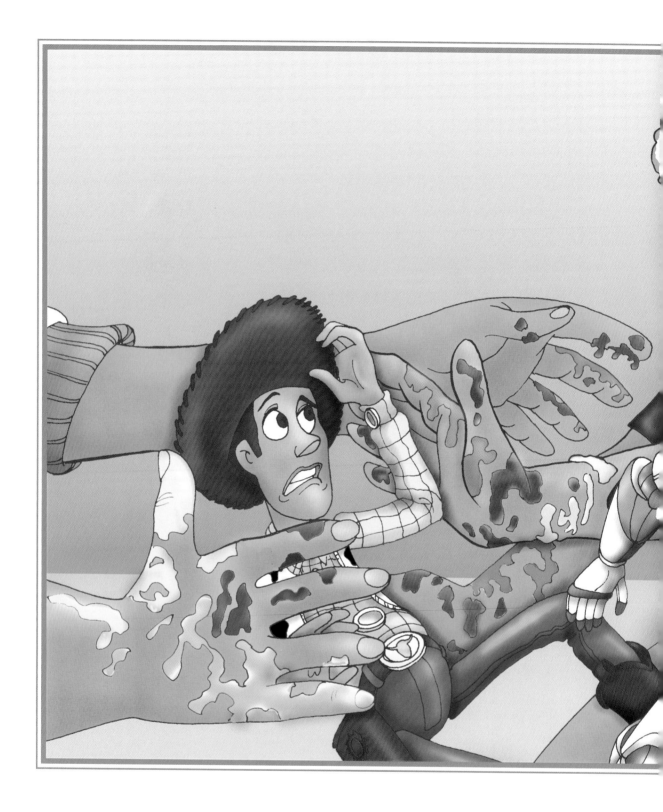

It is kindergarten!"

Kindergarten means finger

paints! Sticky fingers

grabbed Buzz and Woody.

"We have to find Buzz and Woody!" Sarge said. "Let's go to the mess hall!"

A cook saw Sarge and his men.

"Green ants!" she yelled.

She grabbed a big can of bug spray.

"Run for cover!" Sarge yelled.

Buzz and Woody
escaped from kindergarten,
but Buzz saw something
else.

BUZZZZZZZZZZ!

BUZZZZZZZ!

"This robot knows
my name!"
Buzz said.

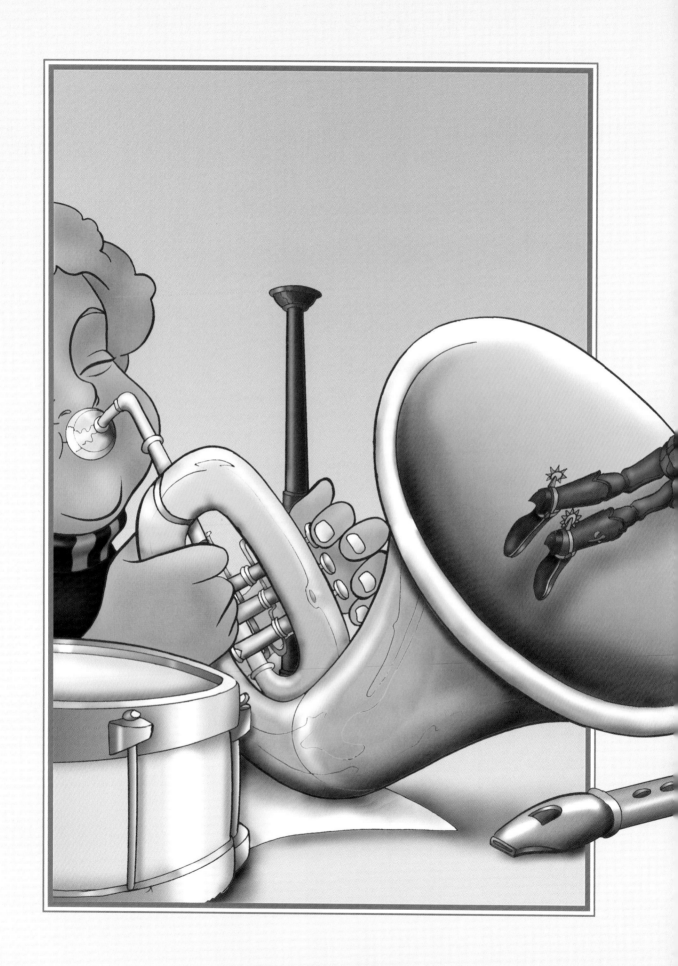

"We have

to hurry,"

said Woody.

But Buzz ran

into the music room.

"This place is fun!"

Buzz yelled.

Buzz and Woody

were blasted out of

a trumpet.

"Let's move, move, move!" Sarge yelled. But the Green Army Men were stuck in glue. Sarge was not happy. Finding Buzz and Woody was not easy!

"We are in a crater," Buzz said.

"It is a water hole!" Woody said.

"Crater!"

"Water hole!"

Water shot out at Buzz.

"You are right, Woody," said Buzz.

"We have to find Andy's cubby," said Woody.

Too late!

A boy grabbed him.

Another boy grabbed Buzz.

"Mine," one boy said.

"No, it's mine," said the other boy.

Buzz and Woody were happy when a teacher stepped in.

"These toys belong to ME now!" she said.

The teacher threw them into her
drawer. They were not alone.

"No toy has escaped this
drawer!" a doll said.

"Now we will really miss show-and-tell!" Woody said.

"Not true, lawman!" yelled Sarge.

The Green Army Men pushed the drawer open.

Buzz and Woody were free!

The toys made it back to Andy's cubby just in time.

"I have one hundred toys for show-and-tell," said Andy.

Buzz and Woody smiled.

Winnie the Pooh

Tiggers Hate to Lose

by Isabel Gaines

One fine spring day,
while bouncing beside the stream,
Tigger found Pooh and his friends
standing on the bridge.

They were all staring into the water.

"What are you doing?" Tigger asked.

"We're playing Pooh Sticks," said Pooh.

"Tiggers love Pooh Sticks!" said Tigger.

"What's Pooh Sticks?"

"It's a game," said Pooh.

"Get some sticks,

and you can play, too."

Tigger found some sticks
and bounced back to the bridge.

"The first stick to pass
under the bridge wins,"
explained Rabbit.
"On your mark, get set . . . go!"

Pooh, Piglet, Rabbit,
Roo, and Eeyore
threw their sticks
into the water.

Tigger decided to watch once
before trying it himself.

Then they all raced
to the other side
of the bridge
to see who had won.

"I can see mine!" Roo shouted.

"I win!"

But just as he said the words,

Roo's "stick" spread its wings

and flew up to join the other dragonflies.

"Can you see yours, Pooh?" Piglet asked.

"No," Pooh replied. "I expect my stick is stuck."

"Look," Rabbit cried.

"There's Eeyore's stick!"

"Oh joy," muttered Eeyore.

"I won."

"Step aside," Tigger said.

"Tiggers are great at Pooh Sticks."

Everyone moved over
so Tigger could play, too.
Once again, Rabbit gave the signal,
"On your mark, get set . . . go!"

They tossed their sticks
off the bridge . . .

. . . then raced to the other side.

Tigger shouted, "Did I win?"

"Nope," mumbled Eeyore. "I did."

"Oh," said Tigger, frowning.
"Well, I was just warming up.
Let's play again."

They played again,
and just like before,
Eeyore's stick sailed past the others.

"Tiggers don't like losing,"
grumbled Tigger.
"Let's play again."

408

Eeyore won the next game, too.

"Oooh, goody," Eeyore said.

"I've won four times in a row."

Eeyore won the next time,
and the next time,
and the time after that, too.
"I just can't lose," muttered Eeyore.

Tigger stamped his foot.

"Let's play again," he said.

"Tiggers *hate* to lose."

During the next game,
at the very last moment,
Eeyore's stick
squeaked by Tigger's.

Tigger threw down his sticks.

"Tiggers don't like Pooh Sticks!"
he cried.

Tigger walked away
with his head down
and no bounce at all.

"I'll tell you my secret,"
Eeyore called.

"You have to drop your stick
in a twitchy sort of way."

Tigger bounced back
to the bridge.
This time when he
dropped his stick,
Tigger made sure to twitch.

And this time,

Tigger's stick won!

Tigger was so happy,

he began bouncing again.

And he bounced right into Eeyore.

The Giving Bear

by Isabel Gaines

"Umph!" grunted Piglet
as he knocked on Pooh's door.
He had his wagon with him.
It was loaded with stuff.

"Hello, Piglet," answered Pooh.

"What's in your wagon?"

"Things from my house,"
Piglet said. "I'm giving them
to Christopher Robin."

Just then Tigger bounced up.

"Hello!" he said.

He had his wagon, too.

"Hello, Tigger," said Pooh.
"Are you giving your things
to Christopher Robin, too?"

"Yes," answered Tigger.

"So he can give them

to someone who needs them."

"Do you have anything
you don't need anymore,
Pooh?" asked Piglet.

"Let me think," said Pooh,
thinking very hard.
But he couldn't think
of a thing.

Along came Christopher Robin.

"I see Piglet's and Tigger's wagons,"
he said. "Are you going
to add anything, Pooh?"

"I don't have anything
to give away," Pooh said sadly.
"There must be something,"
said Tigger.

"Let's look in the cupboard,"
suggested Piglet.

Pooh opened the cupboard doors.

"Oh dear!" said Piglet.

"Zowee!" shouted Tigger.

"Wow!" exclaimed Christopher Robin.

"Twenty honeypots!" they said
at the same time.

"Only ten honeypots

have any honey

in them," Christopher Robin said.

"I keep a large supply
of honeypots at all times,"
said Pooh.

"Why is that, Pooh Bear?"
asked Christopher Robin.
"Just in case," announced Pooh.

"In case of what?" asked Piglet.

He was a little afraid

to hear the answer.

"I might find
some especially
yummy honey," Pooh said.

"I would need plenty of pots
to store it in, so I would
never run out."

"ALL honey tastes
especially yummy to you!"
Christopher Robin
reminded Pooh gently.

"Ten pots are more than enough
to store your yummy honey."

"But what if I had a party?" asked Pooh. "Everyone would want some honey, so I would need a lot."

"Pooh," Christopher Robin said,
"if you had a party, you would
invite your friends in the
Hundred-Acre Wood."

"Ten honeypots hold
more than enough honey
for us," said Piglet.

"Hmm," said Pooh.
He still wasn't sure
he wanted to give away
his honeypots.

"Think of everyone
who could enjoy some honey
if you shared your honeypots,"
said Christopher Robin.

"Then they would all be
as happy as I am!" agreed Pooh.
Pooh decided to give away
ten of his honeypots.
His heart felt twice its size.

"Silly old bear," said Christopher Robin.
He helped Pooh load his honeypots
onto his wagon.

Winnie the Pooh

Eeyore Finds Friends

by Isabel Gaines

One lovely spring morning,
Gopher popped out of a hole
right beside Eeyore.

"Say, sonny," said Gopher,
"why are you alone?
Don't you know
today is *Twos*-day?

"You should be with a friend.
One friend plus one friend
equals *Twos*-day."

"I see," said Eeyore sadly.

Then he perked up.

"Aren't you my friend, Gopher?"

"Of course I am," replied Gopher.
"But I promised to spend the day
with Rabbit. Good-bye, sonny,
and good luck!"

Eeyore thought he would try
his luck with Owl, so he set off
into the woods.

Everywhere Eeyore looked,

he saw animals in pairs.

He saw two chipmunks . . .

and two possums . . .

and two bluebirds.

Eeyore hoped that Owl

was not part of a pair.

But as Eeyore walked
up to Owl's house,
he saw that Owl had a guest.

Owl and Kanga were having
a tea party outside with an iced cake
and everything.

"I get it," Eeyore muttered.

"Tea for two on *Twos*-day.

How nice."

As Eeyore walked away,
he saw two butterflies
fluttering above a flower.

There were two worms

inching along the path.

And two strange creatures
were bouncing in the meadow.

Eeyore noticed that the creatures
were Tigger and Roo.

"I'm no good at bouncing, anyway,"
Eeyore told himself,
watching from behind a tree.

As Eeyore turned away,
he remembered that he had
only two more friends to see.

"Pooh and Piglet are probably
spending *Twos*-day together,"
Eeyore mumbled. "But who knows?
Maybe I'll get lucky."

But as Eeyore suspected,
Piglet was not at home.

Piglet was at Pooh's house.
Eeyore watched the pair
through the window.

"Oh, well," Eeyore sighed.
"I might as well go home
and sleep until *Winds*-day."

Just then Pooh saw Eeyore,
and hurried to the door.

"Hello, Eeyore," Pooh called.

"Would you like to join us for a snack?

We're having my favorite—honey."

"But that would ruin *Twos*-day,"
said Eeyore.

"Today is *Twos*-day?" asked Pooh.
"I forgot."

Pooh scratched his head
and thought. Finally, he said,
"*Twos*-day could *stay* forgotten!

We could call today *Fun*-day, instead.

It rhymes with Monday."

"I see," said Eeyore, though he didn't.

Eeyore followed Pooh inside,
and the three friends had a *Fun*-day,
which was three times as nice
as a *Twos*-day!

Winnie the Pooh

Pooh's Surprise Basket

by Isabel Gaines

The first of May

was a beautiful spring day.

Pooh decided to take a walk.

Pooh loved this time of year.

He sang a tune about it:

"Oh, I love spring.

Dum-dee dum-dum.

It makes me sing.

Pum-dee pum-pum.

"I pick spring flowers.
Dum-dee dum-dum.

I could do that for hours!
Pum-dee pum-pum."

At home, Pooh looked
at all the flowers
he had picked.

"These flowers are so pretty,"
he said.
"I should share them
with my friends."

Pooh got an idea.
"I can surprise everyone
with flower baskets
made just for them."

Pooh got right to work.

Pooh started with Piglet's basket.
He gathered clover and buttercups,
the smallest flowers he had picked.
He put them in the smallest basket.

Pooh held up Piglet's basket and smiled.
"A tiny basket," he said aloud.

"Tigger's turn!" said Pooh.

Pooh tossed a bunch

of flowers in the basket.

They went every which way.

"A messy basket," said Pooh.

For Rabbit, Pooh chose flowers
of the same color.
Carefully, he cut them
all to the same size.

"A neat and tidy basket," he said.

For Roo's basket, Pooh
went to the cupboard.
He pulled out several bouncy balls.
He put them in the basket,
and added some flowers.

"A fun basket!" he said.

Pooh made a pretty basket for Kanga,

a wise basket for Owl,

and an Eeyore basket for Eeyore.

It was full of sticks and stones.

Pooh placed the last basket
on the table. He was ready
to make Christopher Robin's
basket.

He reached for the flowers.

But there was a problem.

NO MORE FLOWERS!

"Oh dear!" cried Pooh.
"What will I put
in Christopher Robin's basket?

"Aha!" Pooh cried.
He tied a red ribbon
around the basket.

Then he gathered up
all the baskets
and ran out of the house.

Pooh left a basket at each
friend's house.
He went to Rabbit's house
and Piglet's house,
Tigger's, Eeyore's, and Owl's.

Then he stopped by
Kanga and Roo's.
He went to Christopher Robin's
house last.

Christopher Robin was outside.
"Christopher Robin," said Pooh,
"I surprised everyone
with flower baskets.

But I wanted to give you
something extra-special."
Pooh sat down inside the basket
and said, "This is a Pooh basket.
I made it just for you!"

"Silly old bear,"
said Christopher Robin.
"You are the best surprise ever!"

Winnie the Pooh

Be Quiet, Pooh!

by Isabel Gaines

The sun streamed in
through Pooh's window.
"What a happy day!" he said.

Pooh got out of bed.

He stretched up.

He stretched down.

Then he ate
a big jar of honey.

It was nice outside,

so Pooh decided to take a walk.

While Pooh walked,
he made up a song.
"I had some honey.
Today is so sunny.
Hum-dee, ho-hummy."

Soon Pooh came
to Rabbit's house.
"Hum-dee-dee
dum-dum," Pooh sang.

Rabbit poked his head
out of his window.
"Pooh, you woke
me up!" said Rabbit.

"I'm sorry," said Pooh.

"Would you like to sing with me?"

"No," said Rabbit.

Rabbit slammed his window shut
and went back to bed.
Pooh continued on his walk.

The next day was also
bright and sunny.
Pooh woke up
in a happy mood.

Pooh got out of bed.

He stretched up.

He stretched down.

Then he ate
a big jar of honey.

Once again,

he went out for a walk.

"The sun is so sunny,

I want more honey," sang Pooh.

When Pooh walked by Rabbit's house,
Pooh saw something new.

"Rabbit has a sign,
and it looks so fine,"
Pooh sang.

"Pooh, you woke me up again!"
shouted a sleepy Rabbit.
"Sorry, Rabbit," said Pooh.
"I like your new sign."

"Thank you," said Rabbit.
"I made it. It says,

NO SINGING IN THE MORNING!"
"You did a very nice job,"
said Pooh.

The next morning,
Pooh decided to walk
in the other direction.

Rabbit slept happily
in his bed until he heard,
"Chirp, chirpety, chirp."
"Is that you, Pooh?" he called.

He looked out his window,
but Pooh was nowhere in sight.
Then Rabbit saw
a bird's nest on the sign.

"Chirp, chirpety, chirp,"
sang the baby birds
in the nest.
"Oh dear," said Rabbit.

He couldn't tell the baby birds
to be quiet.
They were so cute.
Their song was so sweet.

The next morning,
Rabbit awoke once again
to the baby birds' singing.

He tried to be mad at them.

But as he listened to their song,

Rabbit discovered he rather liked it.

Then Rabbit heard Pooh
coming down the path.
Pooh was singing, too.
And his song matched
the baby birds' song.

Rabbit got an idea.

He jumped out of bed
and ran outside.

When Pooh arrived
at Rabbit's house,
he noticed Rabbit's sign
was different.

PLEASE
NO SINGING
IN THE
MORNING

"What happened to your sign?"
asked Pooh.

"I fixed it," said Rabbit.

"Now it says,

PLEASE SING IN THE MORNING."

"What a wonderful idea!"

said Pooh.

"Would you like to join me
in a song or two now?"
"I most certainly would,"
said Rabbit.

And from that day on,
Pooh and Rabbit started every day
with a song.

Winnie the Pooh

Pooh's Scavenger Hunt

by Isabel Gaines

It was a sunny day in the
Hundred-Acre Wood.
Christopher Robin was sitting on a
tree stump when Pooh and all his
friends came to say hello.

"Hello, Christopher Robin," said Pooh.
"What are we going to do today?"

"Why don't we have
a scavenger hunt?"
said Christopher Robin.

"Tiggers love scavenger hunts!"
yelled Tigger.
"What is a scavenger hunt?"

"A scavenger hunt is a game
where you hunt for things,"
said Christopher Robin.

"What kinds of things?" asked Rabbit.
Christopher Robin scratched
his head. "Oh let me think.

Why don't you look for

a purple flower,

a small jar of honey,

and a red leaf?"

Christopher Robin smiled.
"And then,
I want you to find
the greatest thing
in the whole world."

Pooh was confused.

"Isn't honey the greatest thing
in the whole world?"
he asked.

"Honey is great,"
said Christopher Robin.
"But there is something
even greater."

So Pooh and his friends
went into the forest to search.

They went to Pooh's house first,
for that was the best place
to find honey.

"Up there is my only
small jar of honey,"
said Pooh.
"How will we
get it down?"

"Climb on my shoulders,"
said Tigger.

"I still can't reach it," said Pooh.

"Rabbit, can you help?"

"I can't quite reach.
Maybe if Roo helped, too?"
said Rabbit.

Roo grabbed the jar of honey,
and dropped it to Kanga.
Kanga put it in a bag.

"Next we need a leaf
and a flower," said Pooh.
"Does anybody remember
which should be red
and which should be purple?"
No one did.

"Well," said Pooh.

"Here is a red flower.

And it smells nice."

"Then it's perfect," said Kanga.

Everyone agreed.

"I found a leaf,"
Roo called.
"But it is not purple."

"I have some purple paint
at my house," said Rabbit.
"We can paint the leaf purple."
And that's what they did.

"Now all we need
is the greatest thing
in the whole world,"
said Piglet.

They headed back
into the woods.
"Greatest thing," called Pooh,
"where are you?"

They walked and walked.
Soon it grew quite late—
and quite dark.
They all held hands
so no one would get lost.

Finally, they found
Christopher Robin,
sitting on the tree stump.
They were back
where they had started.

"Hello," said
Christopher Robin.
"Are you done with
the scavenger hunt?"

"No," said Pooh sadly.

"We all searched together."

"And found everything," said Tigger.

"Except for the greatest thing
in the whole world,"
said Rabbit.

Christopher Robin smiled.
"But you did! You found
the greatest thing in the
whole world."

"We did?" they all asked.
"Oh yes. You searched
together," said
Christopher Robin.

"Friends working together
is the greatest thing
in the whole world.
I knew you would find it!"